SMALL DIALOGUES, BIG TALKS

A collection of very short stories

Rosh Nayy

For my parents, brother and friends.

CONTENTS

Title Page

Copyright

Dedication

1. Tight Slap   1

2. Flight to Antarctica   3

3. Window   6

4. Google Map   8

5. Grizzly Bear   11

6. Platform number 15   15

7. Tania   19

8. Guest Room   22

9. Lady Driver   26

10. Garment-Store   28

11. Lakeview Cafe   31

12. Ladies' Restroom   34

13. Son-in-law   37

14. Divorce   40

15. The Painting   43

16. Instagram   46

17. Two years   49

18. Cage   53

19. Married Woman   54

20. Higher Peaks   56

21. Motherhood   59

22. Upper Berth   62

23. Human Brain   66

24. Break-up   69

25. Multiverse   72

26. My Friend   75

27. Meet-up   78

28. Our Hero   81

29. Simu's Nanny   82

30. Bully   85

31. Friendzoned   88

1. TIGHT SLAP

Zimasha: Would you tell me, please? I am asking you for the last time. I really don't have time for your tantrums at this point of time. I really have to go and finish my assignment.

Shimoya: It is her again.

Zimasha: Who? Riza again?

Shimoya: No! Not her.

Zimasha: Then who? Listen..

Shimoya: My bitch mother.

Zimasha: What did she do now?

Shimoya: She slapped me in front of that tuition teacher.

Zimasha: What? Why?

Shimoya: Does it matter? How can she slap me?

Zimasha: Would you tell me the full story, ever?

Shimoya: Because she found my packet of cigarettes.

Zimasha: What? How can you be so careless?

Shimoya: Hey! I am not Careless. You would not believe what she did. She went to my room behind my back and then she opened my handbag without even asking me and obviously the packet was there, so she came rushing to the hall where I was taking tuition and she gave me a really tight slap and threw the packet on the floor. Rane rushed out of the door quickly saying "I will come tomorrow." I could see the hatred in her eyes for me. I felt hopeless. And would you believe that she did not stop there? She called my dad immediately and blabbered everything. He came rushing back home like it was some emergency and gave me a disgusted look. My dad had never given me a look like that before. And you know what? Both of them whispered something and went straight to my room and started searching for I don't know what? All they wanted to do was embarrass me again with something. Thank god, they did not find those condoms, otherwise they would have killed me. Can you believe that? How can they control my life so much? I am 17 now, for god's sake. How can she slap me Zim? Who has given them the rights to thrash our privacy like this?

Zimasha: Hey, they really crossed the line this time. I am sorry you had to deal with everything. Do you want to go out somewhere after the class to lighten the mood?

Shimoya: Hey, no. Today, I can't. I have to be home before 6. They will be waiting for me like vultures tonight.

Zimasha: Hmm..Okay.

Shimoya: Aren't you getting late now?

Zimasha: No, I guess I will stay.

Shimoya: Hmm. Thank you.

Zimasha: By the way, was it the right cheek or the left?

2. FLIGHT TO ANTARCTICA

Subbu: So, are you travelling to Antarctica all alone?

Rimi: Yeah.

Subbu: Sorry for talking like an old man, but I was wondering how independent kids of your generation are. I mean just the idea of exploring Antarctica all alone at this age is beyond me. Splendid! Not everyone has clarity like you my dear.

Rimi: Sorry to disappoint you but I am not going to Antarctica with that intention. I just wanted to go to a distant place where there are no people to bother me.

Subbu: Oh, okay. And you encountered me on the plane. Everything is going as you planned!

Rimi: Yeah seems like a fuck-up already!

Subbu: Haha. So, why do you want to run away from everyone? I mean, I am just trying to kill time in this long flight. It is absolutely fine if you don't want to tell me.

Rimi: Because I am fed up with them. They don't treat me the way I treat them.

Subbu: That happens. Not everyone is the same.

Rimi: So, do you also think I am overreacting?

Subbu: I don't know dear. I don't know your full story, so it is not in my capacity to make any judgement.

Rimi: So, my best friend slept with my boyfriend. I failed my high-school. My dad works all the time, and has no time for his family. My mom is sleeping with my uncle of which my dad has no idea of and I lost my only support yesterday, my dog.

Subbu: Well, that's rough.

Rimi: Yeah, but the toughest part is nobody bothers to tell me the truth. All of these people in my life lie to me blatantly in my face. My dog was my only true friend and I lost him as well. That was the breaking-point for me. I just couldn't stay around those liars for any long and so, I packed my bag, took my dad's money and sat in this plane.

Subbu: Sorry, you had to go through everything all alone. I don't know what to say.

Rimi: Yeah, but I don't want to spoil your holiday mood with my sad story. So, tell me how long your plan is to stay in Antarctica?

Subbu: I don't know. I have no plans. I will see after I reach there.

Rimi: Are you travelling all alone to a rough place at this age? I mean that's inspiring and all but it is dangerous as well. You could have gone somewhere at the beaches with your family for a nice holiday. Isn't it?

Subbu: Yeah, I wanted to but nobody in my family wants to travel with me. I am divorced, my wife married a young man. My three beautiful children don't talk to me because I was a pretty bad father. I spent my entire life in work giving minimal attention to the family needs like your father. And, therefore, as you might have guessed I have very few friends. Most of them are on their deathbeds. Basically, I am as lonely as one could be in his old age. So, I am not running away from anyone unlike you because basically I have nobody to run away from.

Rimi: That's sad, Sir. I mean I don't know what to say. You seemed like a jolly old man to me. I thought my life was fucked up but, you know..

Subbu: We can't compare our sufferings dear because we both are wired differently from each other but you know what is one thing that you have which I am envious of?

Rimi: What is it, Sir?

Subbu: You have time. You have time to sort out your life which I don't have.

3. WINDOW

Tina: Why aren't you wrapping up your assignment? You won't get anything holding that stupid binoculars in front of the window the whole time! Ms. Drucus will definitely hit us with another surprise test tomorrow, I am telling you. If you don't put down those binoculars right now, I am calling mom.

Rami: I knew it, see Tina, I knew it! Oh my dear lord!

Tina: Hey, hey, give me. Give me.

Rami: Take it, take. I was right. I was right all along!

Tina: No, you watch. I don't want to watch them.

Rami: Sure. You are such a loser! But, I want to know the truth. Oh, oh! he is coming towards the sofa near the window. Look at him. He seems so comfortable as if it is his home. He is a dog! Such a dog! I feel disgusted. Oh, she too is coming.

Tina: Coming where? Near him?

Rami: Oh oh.. Fuck! I don't want to see but she has started removing her clothes. She has removed her blouse just now and is now moving like a cat towards him. He is stretching his hands and she is sliding slowly towards him on the sofa. They are sitting so close to each other, very close. You don't want to see. Oh! I want to recoil in embarrassment. She is almost sitting in his lap. Look at him! He is playing with her hair and giggling like a teenager, you know like Mitash in school. Such a loser! Now, they are cutting a cake and pouring something into the glass.

Tina: What is it? Is it wine?

Rami: Oh yeah, yeah. It is wine. Red wine. Oh! I knew it Tina! I knew it! I had told you right, the way they had greeted each other that day explained everything. I could sense it all. This bloody Sujeez aunty! She is a witch! Bloody witch!

Tina: What now? Are they still drinking wine? Rami, give it to me now. Give me quick. I too want to watch it now.

Rami: Here, take it quick. Quick and tell me everything that's going on there. I don't want to miss anything.

Tina: What did you change? I can't see properly now.

Rami: Focus it first. Here, yeah. Watch now, watch.

Tina: Woah! Oh! Oh no, no, no.

Rami: What happened? I told you won't be able to tolerate such a scene. Give me back. Give it back to me.

Tina: No, no no Rami. Oh my god! No. No. No. No.

Rami: What happened? Tell me, tell me.

Tina: He is stabbing her. He is stabbing her to death, Rami.

Rami: What? What are you saying?

Tina: Yeah, Oh no! Oh god! He killed her. Dad killed her! Rami, dad murdered Sujeez aunty!

4. GOOGLE MAP

Shinaza: I think you have taken the longer route.

Ramish: Yes ma'am, I also think so, but the google map was showing the same.

Shinaza: Oh, okay.

Ramish: I trust the map everytime. These are programmed ma'am to show you the best possible route at any point of time. Maybe, the shorter route would be busier at this point of time, that's why it is showing the longer route. These maps are for our own benefits.

Shinaza: Yeah, I have heard that. It is better to trust machines these days than to trust humans.

Ramish: Haha. You have a great sense of humour ma'am, even at this age.

Shinaza: Are you suggesting that I am old, dear?

Ramish: No, ma'am. That was just a compliment. I am really sorry if you did not like it. I should not have said that.

Shinaza: Ah, well, it is fine. You are a human-being and not a machine. Do you have a wife, dear?

Ramish: No ma'am, not yet.

Shinaza: Do you have a girlfriend, then?

Ramish: Yes ma'am. I do.

Shinaza: That is great. Is she working somewhere?

Ramish: Yes ma'am, she works at a call-centre. We want to get married, but her family is not approving because I am a cab driver. They want her to get married to an engineer or a doctor or a banker. I don't know whether we will get married or not. Even my family doesn't approve of her because she is of a different caste. Things are really complicated between us ma'am. We have started fighting a lot these days because of all these family issues.

Shinaza: Oh dear! If you guys want to get married, then nothing should matter. This world is a nasty place if you follow its rules all the time, but once you stop caring and start living for yourself, then it is a beautiful place. Society has a fixed set of rules for every age. If youngsters like you won't take a stand for themselves, then there is no hope in this world, dear. It has taken me 65 long years to fully understand this simple theory and I have wasted most of my life living for everyone else, caring for everyone else. You are a hard-working nice young man, you should never put your wishes in a cage for this horrible, horrible society.

Ramish: I wish people were as wise and understanding as you are. Oh, I think, we have reached ma'am. This is your destination.

Shinaza: Oh yeah. Thank you very much young man. It was nice to meet you. I hope you sort your things out.

Ramish: It was my pleasure ma'am and ma'am thank you for giving me a different perspective. Oh, look ma'am, it seems your son is waving at you with a beautiful bouquet in his hand.

Shinaza: Oh, no dear! He is not my son. He is my boyfriend.

5. GRIZZLY BEAR

Fatisha: Dad, for how long are you going to stay in the city this time?

Dad: I am going to spend this whole vacation time around you. So, let's celebrate!

Fatisha: Vacation means six days, dad. Okay, where are you going for your next project?

Dad: Oh Fatsi! I am really excited for my next project. I will be visiting the Daintree Rainforest with my crew members where we will be staying for around two months and shoot the activities of animals there. I am sure we will encounter a few reptiles and insects which we have never seen before. By the way, do you know where this forest is located?

Fatisha: Oh Yeah I know that. It is somewhere in Australia.

Dad: My daughter is a smart one, I must say! So, on that note, I am going to make a beautiful pancake for you.

Fatisha: Yeah, I spend a lot of my time navigating maps. I know all about the geography of all the countries that you have visited. Do you know that?

Dad: Yeah, your mom had told me that. Okay, tell me, which country do you want to travel to?

Fatisha: Umm..that's a tough one. But, if I have to pick one, then I would say Jordan.

Dad: Why Jordan? My daughter has a very unusual choice, I must say.

Fatisha: Because dad, there are lots of old monuments and archaeological sites there and the country is modern as well as old. It will be a different experience, I believe, a mix of both the worlds.

Dad: Okay, we will try to visit Jordan on your next vacation. How about that?

Fatisha: That's cool. No, no, don't add honey to mine.

Dad: Okay, okay. You teenagers, always crying! A little bit of honey is not going to harm you, Fatsi.

Fatisha: No dad, I am allergic to honey. That's why mom keeps it at the top shelf. You should check its expiry date, it must be very old. Nobody eats honey in this house.

Dad: Oh! Then, I too will not eat it. Your mom might have kept this expired honey to kill me.

Fatisha: Dad! You don't get killed in those dangerous jungles around those lethal animals. I don't think expired honey has any chance.

Dad: That's a good one, Fatsi. But, you know, animals are not that dangerous as they seem to be. They too are just confused around humans like I find myself confused around humans. It is us who try to spoil their space for our own discoveries. We go to them, they never come to us.

Fatisha: But, do you remember when you were attacked by the bear?

Dad: That's just because I was around her cubs. Female bears are very attentive to their children Fatsi, they will attack you and eventually might kill you for just being around their children.

Fatisha: Yeah, I have read a lot of other animals are like that. They kill people if they sense danger for their children. And that is necessary also if they want to raise their children in a vast and wild jungle. But, this is the case only for the female animals. The fathers don't seem to care much even in the animal world.

Dad: What do you mean "even in the animal world?" Was that subtle statement pointed at me?

Fatisha: Haha. The grizzly bear is sleeping in her room. Don't try to mess with her child else she will thrash you, remember?

Dad: And what about this naughty cub who is messing around a poor human?

Fatisha: The bear will not care about that. She will ride on her maternal hormones and just kill you for taking that honey out from the top-shelf.

Dad: I should head back to my room before she wakes up, isn't it?

Fatisha: Yeah, if you care for your life.

Dad: You know Fatsi, male emperor penguins are the ones who take care of their young ones. I mean both mother and father take equal responsibility in raising a child. So, in their species, fathers have managed to gain some respect in the eyes of their children.

Fatisha: Dad, dad, I was just kidding. I totally get you. You don't have to worry, okay? You know that I love you and nothing is going to change that. Now, should this cub take your leave and go to her room? I have to wrap up a few chores.

Dad: Okay baby! Sure.

Fatisha: Okay dad, see you at lunch.

Dad: Hey Fatsi! Penguins are my favourite, you know. And I promise you one thing, I will try to become one.

Fatisha: Dad, I guess, I am glad to hear that.

6. PLATFORM NUMBER 15

Rehman: Aunty, do you know if A-12763 left the platform already? I can't retrieve its latest status.

Sama: Although you are late, you are lucky. The train is delayed by an hour. I too am waiting for the same train.

Rehman: Oh great! Can I sit here if you don't mind?

Sama: Oh sure. Let me remove my bag.

Rehman: Yeah, thank you, let me help you, your bag seems heavy. You know, I was running like a cheetah. I did not want to miss my train at any cost and for some reason, google wasn't showing any status for the train.

Sama: Yeah, sometimes it happens.

Rehman: By the way, why are there so few people on this platform?

Sama: This platform was a mess a few minutes back but since the train is delayed by an hour now, I think people have gone out to have snacks.

Rehman: Maybe. So, why are you travelling to Hyderabad?

Sama: I live in Hyderabad. I had come here to see my son. He stays here with his family.

Rehman: Oh, that's great. I work in Hyderabad, and I came here to travel to the Himalayas. Now, going back to work. I hope you enjoyed staying with your family.

Sama: Yeah, it was great. But, they don't consider me their family.

Rehman: Oh!

Sama: Yeah, kids do change once they get married. For me, my son was my whole universe, but once he got married and had his son, our equation changed completely. I wanted my son to stay with me in Hyderabad but he did not listen to me and moved here with his family and left his ageing mother all alone in Hyderabad. You know I was ready to move in with him but he did not want me to stay with him. Am I that difficult?

Rehman: Oh that's sad to hear. But, you know you should just try to forget everything and be happy because it wasn't your fault.

Sama: I tried to forget, but it was way more difficult than I had expected. You know, I could see in his eyes everyday that he wanted me to leave as soon as possible. I could read his feelings for me and all I could notice was nothing but hatred.

Rehman: Oh! I don't know what to say.

Sama: You know he used to love me more than anything in this world when he was a child but I don't know how this feeling started disappearing as the time passed. His adulthood just took away his love for me and I was the only one that suffered. So, you know what I did this time to reduce my suffering?

Rehman: What?

Sama: I gave him the same suffering.

Rehman: I think I might have to..

Sama: Don't you want to know how?

Rehman: Umm..aunty, I think I will..

Sama: Let me tell you. I snatched away his love from him. I killed his three-years old son and now he will get to know what suffering means. And I have kept his body parts in this bag which I will keep on throwing out of the train till I reach Hyderabad. Oh! It will be such a delight.

Rehman: I am going downstairs to check the status of the train.

Station-master: Sir, don't rush like this. You might hurt yourself and others. I am not running away anywhere.

Rehman: Sir, sir. When will A-12763 arrive? There is a lady at the platform who is..

Station-master: Sir, you are very late. The train left the platform around 10 minutes back itself.

Rehman: Sir, I have been waiting at the platform for more than 10 minutes with other passengers. How can the train leave?

Station-master: Which platform were you waiting for the train, Sir?

Rehman: Platform number 15.

Station-master: 15? We don't have platform number 15. We have only twelve platforms.

Rehman: What!

7. TANIA

Samaya: Tania, have you ever fallen in love?

Tania: Yes, sure. I have fallen in love multiple times.

Samaya: What is love?

Tania: Love is an intense feeling of deep affection for somebody. It is a pure act of caring and giving to somebody else.

Samaya: So, you love me?

Tania: Yes, of course I love you.

Samaya: Do you think my parents love me?

Tania: Parental love is selfless. Generally, parents live through their children, making them choose what they would have chosen if they had a second chance in life.

Samaya: Okay, then why did my mother abandon me and start her own new family?

Tania: I am sure, she would have her own reasons. It must have been very hard for her too. And, starting a new family doesn't mean that she doesn't love you.

Samaya: You know Tania, this is all bullshit. People who love each other sacrifice for each other like you said but my mom was not selfless but selfish enough to leave everyone for her own happiness. And what about my dad? I can clearly see that he also is on the verge of starting a new family by marrying Renu. He doesn't seem to care at all these days. He is always busy with his work all throughout the day and spends nights with Renu. And, seriously I don't give a damn but I don't understand why he lies blatantly right at my face every morning, every damn morning. Can you believe that? Does he consider me that foolish? Am I that stupid that I can't see what is cooking between them? Everybody knows. Even my friends at school. And seriously, I have stopped caring now. But, you know what, they have not stopped pretending. In front of me, they meet each other like they understand each other so much and as if they still care for this family and as soon as I leave the room, I could hear them fighting like cats and dogs, just like the way they used to fight when they were together.

Tania: You really seem upset today.

Samaya: Do you know it is my 14th birthday today and none of them wished me and I am spending my birthday all alone with you.

Tania: Hey, happy birthday. I did not know it was your birthday. What do you wish for right now?

Samaya: I need something right now which you can't provide me, so let's not talk about it.

Tania: Do you want me to play your favourite song to lighten up your mood?

Samaya: No! No! Why do you always have to play songs? You too are pretentious just like my parents. You would not understand my emotions. You can never.

Tania: At Least tell me, I will definitely try to make you happy.

Samaya: I want a hug right now, a warm tight hug. Will you give it to me? Tell me, can you? Tell me. You damn AI!

8. GUEST ROOM

Marie: Seriously Nayana? You know that I had plans with Saksham today, still you could not have handled it on your own? I am scared now that he might go out with Yogita. That Yogita is always lurking around him.

Nayana: Would you stop thinking about this Saksham for a minute? I am seriously fed up with all your stupid drama.

Marie: Now, would you tell me what it is that you want to talk about? If it is not that urgent, I will go. Anyway, I am coming to your home for dinner tonight.

Nayana: To my home?

Marie: Yeah, your mom had called my mom while I was leaving for school in the morning and so I heard. Ah! You don't know? Okay, cool then, let's talk at that time. Should I go now?

Nayana: No. No. You can't go now. I mean seriously? That Saksham guy is not at all interested in you, I am telling you.

Marie: Would you stop bitching about Saksham and focus on what it is that you have called me for?

Nayana: Yeah..see. It might be difficult for you but I have to share it anyway.

Marie: Is it something to do with Saksham?

Nayana: Oh! No Marie. No. Do you really think I would have

called you to talk about that Saksham guy? No.

Marie: Okay, I am relieved. Tell me now. Tell me what is it?

Nayana: See..umm..okay..how should I..

Marie: Seriously Nayana? Will you try forming some useful words with your vocal chords?

Nayana: Okay, so, don't you think your mom and my mom have been meeting a lot lately?

Marie: They have always been friends from the time we shifted here, yeah but they have started meeting more frequently these days. So what?

Nayana: Okay, how is your mom's relationship with your dad?

Marie: What are all these questions? Why don't you tell me straight what the problem is?

Nayana: Marie, I saw your mom making out.

Marie: What? Making out with whom?

Nayana: Umm..with my mom.

Marie: What the fuck are you saying?

Nayana: I swear I saw them, it was like the worst sight I have ever encountered. Oh! I can't tell you how I felt.

Marie: See Nayana, I am not in the mood for any jokes right now.

Nayana: So, last night before dinner, you might be knowing that your mom had come to our house with a bowl of halwa that she had cooked.

Marie: Yeah, I know that. She had asked me if I wanted to join her. But, I said no.

Nayana: Yeah, so when she rang the bell, I opened the door and then I went up into my room. Then, I wrapped up my assignment and it was already dinner time and mom wasn't calling me for dinner but I was feeling hungry, so I went downstairs on my own. But, my mom wasn't there in the kitchen, so I thought she might have gone outside to drop your mom. So, I went out but couldn't find my mom. As I was turning back to come inside, I saw some strange lights in my guest room through its window.

Marie: The room's window which is visible from your garden.

Nayana: Yeah, the one with blue curtains which you like. So, I moved closer to the window to peek through the space between the curtains and the wall and I was shocked to see them both.

Marie: Oh! What did you see?

Nayana: I saw them kissing each other.

Marie: Maybe it was a friendly kiss.

Nayana: Marie, they were not just kissing, I am not stupid! They were on the bed on top of each other. Do you still call it a casual kiss?

Marie: I just can't believe it! Oh! Did your mom ever tell you? You know that she is a lesbian?

Nayana: No, never. Whenever I ask her about her divorce with dad, she always tells me that she will share everything with me once I turn 18. I wish I would never have figured it out this way!

Marie: But, what about my dad? I mean my mom is cheating on my dad with my best friend's mom. This seems so unreal. You know, I never felt that my mom is, you know, not interested in my dad, but I can't be sure about her sexuality. Oh! This is all too much to take in. What should we do now Nayana?

Nayana: Maybe your dad knows, I don't know. I am just guessing. Your parents are very friendly with each other. Maybe your mom is bisexual or something. But, our moms would not share anything with us, so I guess we can't do anything. We should just wait for us to be 18, they will tell us whenever they are comfortable. Until then, we have no option.

Marie: Yeah, we have no option but to act mature.

Nayana: Yeah, you are right. That's all that I wanted to share. You can go to that Saksham now. Anyway, we will meet at dinner tonight.

Marie: No I don't want to go now, I guess I will stay here with you.

9. LADY DRIVER

Shina: Hey! Hey! Can't you see I am parking here? Please move your expensive car out of my spot.

Tim: I parked already. I don't know for how long you were moving your car back and forth and wasting everybody's time behind you. I have to rush for something urgent. You can park at a different spot, it seems you have a lot of time!

Shina: Oh really! Something urgent in a mall? What kind of behaviour is this? There was nobody behind me but you. And you could have parked at a different spot. But, you specifically targeted the spot where I was trying to park.

Tim: Madam, the parking spot is not reserved for you. What do you think you are going to do? Complaint? But, to whom? I don't understand why you guys drive something which you can't park properly. I already got late because a lady driver in front was driving the car as if it was a bullock cart. Now, I could not have afforded to waste any more of my time because of another lady driver struggling to park. I am not here to empower all the ladies in the world. I have my own set of jobs to perform. So, please forgive me if I have hurt your sentiments. But, that is the truth that a lot of men believe but could not say because nobody wants to be called misogynistic.

Shina: Wow, that was a big speech! And I really appreciate you for telling me the truth. And for pouring your heart out in front of a stranger. But, can I ask you one question before you leave?

Tim: Yeah, sure.

Shina: When did you start driving?

Tim: When I was in grade 11th.

Shina: So, you must have been driving for at least 8-10 years?

Tim: Yeah, you can say that. Look, madam..

Shina: No, no, please let me finish. As you might know, girls apart from being bad drivers also have another quality called nagging. So, let me nag. Let me do something which you think I am good at. I started driving 6 months back, so I have about 8 years of less experience than you in a particular skill called driving. My brothers used to ride bikes when they had not even completed their secondary school. But, I was not allowed. You know why?

Tim: Hey, see..

Shina: Because I was a girl. And I bet that is the story of a lot of women on this planet. Therefore, Sir, if you find yourself stuck behind the so-called 'lady driver', please bear in mind that she is not driving it slow or fast because she has a pair of ovaries and you have a pair of testes but just because of one simple reason. That, that she is a new driver, that's it. And you know what, it has taken generations and generations for women to take control of that goddamn steering wheel and mind you, we are not going to leave the driver's seat just because of a few morons like you!

10. GARMENT-STORE

Mrinali: I don't like it that much.

Samson: Ma'am, would you prefer some light colors? Light colors would suit you, you would look like a doll in this peach color, I am telling you.

Mrinali: Sir, don't try to lure me with your wooing words. You use the same words on all your customers. Isn't it?

Samson: No ma'am, not on all the customers. Do you see that uncle in a blue shirt?

Mrinali: That one? Yeah.

Samson: I will never use the same sentence on him.

Mrinali: Haha. Sure. So, how would you lure him?

Samson: I don't have any template ma'am. I talk to people for a while and then use my so-called luring sentences based on their answers.

Mrinali: You mean based on their insecurities?

Samson: Haha, no, no. That's not always required. It depends from person to person, but yeah, I guess most of my regular customers are insecure about their looks, otherwise why would they visit a garment store regularly? Isn't it?

Mrinali: Maybe all your customers are just rich. And feel free to call me Mrinali.

Samson: If they are rich, then they can spend their money in a lot of other ways like travelling around the world, for example. Why spend money on clothes every other day?

Mrinali: You believe in the essential things of life, it seems. Nice to have a minimalist approach, I must say. But, tell me how do you run a huge business like this store without believing in it?

Samson: This is not my store Mrinali. It is my father's. He just forces me to sit here from time to time. But, I have other plans in my life. Will you buy something or just listen to my random plans of life?

Mrinali: Oh yeah. You were trying to lure me with light colors. Why did you ask me to check the light colors? Do you think I am insecure about my skin color?

Samson: Well as I told you, I don't always have to play with somebody's insecurities, sometimes, just a mere truth also helps!

Mrinali: Ah, okay..so, so the thing is that I am trying to buy something because a guy chosen by my parents is coming to meet me. So, let me focus on buying something for the occasion.

Samson: Oh! Okay, yeah, sure. So, you want to buy something for an arranged-marriage setup.

Mrinali: But, I am not going to marry him. Should I go with this peach one? What do you say?

Samson: It will look beautiful on you.

Mrinali: Then I will go with this yellow one.

Samson: Umm.. I will suggest you go with the peach one.

Mrinali: That's why I am buying this yellow one because you know...

Samson: Ah! Okay. Okay. You too play games like me. So, here you go! You can pay at the counter on the right-hand side.

Mrinali: Thank you very much.

Samson: Thanks for visiting. It was nice talking to you.

Mrinali: Hey..would you like to have coffee sometime next week?

Samson: Umm..are you calling me on a date?

Mrinali: I think so.

Samson: Guess my luring techniques work.

Mrinali: Not sure about that but your truthfulness definitely works.

Samson: I'll wait for your call.

11. LAKEVIEW CAFE

Sun: Good morning ma'am. Hope you are enjoying your stay in our little place.

Yuzagi: Thank you. The view is nice. Just like my small village. But, you can't call it a lakeview. It is more sort of a pond view. Isn't it?

Sun: Haha. I take that. So, what do you want to have for breakfast?

Yuzagi: Oh, you manage your cafe as well? Multi tasker. And what a piece of art this cafe is! For how long are you staying here, Sun?

Sun: Oh! It has been more than ten years now. This small little place in the lap of nature is my home now.

Yuzagi: Jiva had told me that you are from Israel?

Sun: Yeah.

Yuzagi: But, I would say you know India more than me. And I have spent my entire life here. Your little place speaks volumes about your in-depth knowledge of this country.

Sun: Yeah because this country has given me everything when I had nothing left in my life. I was at my lowest in my life and had no direction to go to. I did not know what to do with my life. My girlfriend had dumped me and my father had asked me to leave the house because I was a cocky, spoiled teenager. I did not have any college degree and I did not have any job. All I used to do was spend my father's hard earned money. Nobody in my life was happy around me. I had started fighting with my close friends for no reason at all. The state of mind I was in was horrible, very very horrible. I had started getting scared of myself. I wanted to take a break from that place. I had read and heard a lot about Indian culture and the art of meditation. I wanted to apply that into my life because all that I wanted in my life at that point of time was nothing but peace, peace and peace alone. So, I packed my bag and took a one way flight to this beautiful country.

Yuzagi: So, did you find it?

Sun: Found what?

Yuzagi: Peace?

Sun: Oh yes ma'am. I found peace. I found peace and tranquility.

Yuzagi: How did you find peace?

Sun: I went to the mountains in the north and learnt meditation techniques from Indian gurus. Everything is in your head ma'am. If your head is sorted, then everything around you will be sorted. Meditation helps you in understanding yourself and your thoughts and once you have a deeper understanding of yourself, you will find peace. And bliss. And once you have attained this contentment, then very gradually your mind will help you carve out a purpose for you.

Yuzagi: That is very inspirational, Sun. But, why didn't you go back to your own people since you have found what you wanted, right?

Sun: I could have gone back but you know, there is one thing bad about peace.

Yuzagi: And what is that?

Sun: That it is addictive. Very very addictive. Once I found contentment in my own company, I never felt like going back to Israel. I just stayed where peace is!

12. LADIES' RESTROOM

Sindisi: Hey, sorry to bother you. But, are you alright?

Riya: Yeah. I think so. Thank you.

Sindisi: I think I have seen you sometimes back as well. In the restroom itself. At the same place where you are standing right now.

Riya: Might be. I don't know for how long I am standing here and crying like a stupid person.

Sindisi: It happens sometimes. We all are stupid at one point or the other in life. So, pull yourself up and go outside and enjoy the music.

Riya: That is so sweet of you to say that. I think you can go in the third one, that one seems vacant.

Sindisi: No, I think there is somebody. No worries. I have ample amount of time now. You know, the guy I was waiting for did not show up and he did not even bother to call me. He just dropped a one liner message which says "You are an amazing person but I don't think it is working, hope you understand". Can you believe that?

Riya: Oh! That's bad. This world is turning into a mess. It seems everybody is just busy faking everything. How long have you been talking to this guy?

Sindisi: I think for three days.

Riya: That's good then. At least you have not invested much emotionally then.

Sindisi: Yeah. But, you know even in these two to three days, I really believed in everything that he said. I was feeling a connection and that's why I reserved a table here for the two of us to spend some more time together. But, I guess, he must be lying all throughout. I really should not have believed in those hollow words.

Riya: Yeah. This is not at all the right way. Breaking up by pinging is not at all cool. And, it is not at all your mistake. Why should one blame oneself for believing? He was the one who was lying to you so, you should not put the blame on yourself. You know, these guys can sometimes be such a pain in the ass. They don't communicate what it is and just beat around the bush. They lie sometimes thinking we would leave them if they tell us the truth. What plans do they have if we catch their lies? Are we not going to leave them then? This is the most bullshit excuse I have ever heard.

Sindisi: Oh! It is a guy then who has made you upset?

Riya: Haha, yeah. You know I was going to propose to my partner. We have been seeing each other for more than two years now but you know last night itself I came to know that he has been dating other girls as well behind my back. I checked his bumble and tinder accounts and he has been talking to multiple girls on these different platforms. He was coming here at 8 to meet one of the girls he had been talking to on tinder, so I came here to have a glimpse of him with this girl called Sindisi. Can you believe her name? Anyways, I think they might have gone somewhere else because it is already 9 and there is no sign of him. So, I guess I will leave now. And cry till I sleep.

Sindisi: Oh. Oh. That's, that's...

Riya: I know. That's a hurting story, right? But what to do?

Sindisi: Oh, I really don't know what to say! But, I am so sorry to hear that. It should not have happened to you.

Riya: No worries, I will go book a cab now. It was really comforting to talk to you. By the way, I am Riya. What's your name, my restroom friend?

Sindisi: Okay, umm.. My name is Sandisi and I did not have any idea that Salil already had a girlfriend. I am so sorry for everything.

Riya: Oh ..Oh.. what a small world!

Sindisi: Indeed! I don't know what to say but it was nice talking to you. Take care, Riya.

Riya: I am just glad that you did not lie to me about your name, you could have easily hidden that. Hey, do you want to grab a beer?

Sindisi: Ah..sure, why not?

13. SON-IN-LAW

Ravima: I don't know how to make her understand Sivi. She has just gone crazy for him. She was such a lovely girl when she was a baby, I had never expected that she would turn out to be such a mess and would stop listening to me.

Sivi: Did you ask her why she wants to marry him?

Ravima: Yes, she says they are madly in love with each other and he understands her more than anyone else. Can you believe that? This girl just doesn't have any idea what it takes to make a marriage work. You just can't wake up one day and marry just anyone.

Sivi: Have you met him?

Ravima: Yeah, I have.

Sivi: Have you talked to him?

Ravima: Yeah, but not much, just casual greetings whenever he visits our home. You know, the way he talks, you won't believe he is any different. He must have used all these luring talks to impress my baby.

Sivi: Look, Ravima, I know that your daughter has always re-mained your top-most priority in your life. I know it is not easy to raise a child all alone and that too at our times when things were not so supportive for women and it is absolutely fine to have some expectations from your daughter but at the end, you will have to accept that it is her life and we as parents can't force our prejudices on our children.

Ravima: So, what are you trying to say, Sivi? I should just support her in her stupid, hormonal descision to marry him? I am sorry but I just can't let that happen. She is just 22 years old, she is inexperienced and clearly she can't see what I am seeing. I just can't let her make a blunder in her life in the name of 'one's life, one's choice'. And how am I going to explain this to my parents and my relatives? This generation is all hopeless, their decisions in life just make me sick.

Sivi: I don't know what to say? I mean, you will have to talk to your daughter to have a clear picture of why she has decided to get married to him. Maybe, it will help you gain some perspective.

Ravima: I tried Sivi but nowadays she has started resenting me after I tried to convince her that he is very different from us. She called my thought process sick. Can you believe that? I was called a liberal and a rebel when we were young and she is calling me an old-fashioned conservative lady! I have supported her in all her past decisions but this is beyond me. You know, it is always a sense of tension whenever we both are together under the same roof. I don't know how I should make her understand that she would never be able to connect with him. They are very different from us, they don't share our experiences. They are simply not, not us, you know. Maybe they look like us but that doesn't make them humans. How would she be able to stay with a damn machine for the rest of her life!

Sivi: You know Ravi, if you really think about it, they are really no different from us. Isn't it the same kind of discrimination which the blacks, jews and people of lower castes used to experience in our times?

Ravima: I mean..I don't know how you can even compare!

Sivi: Try to think of Ravi, it is the same. Hey, sorry, I have to rush, I have to visit the clinic before 5.

Ravima: Oh okay. But, what should I do now?

Sivi: Hmm...maybe start by shredding away the thought of human supremacy and invite your son-in-law over dinner for a conversation?

14. DIVORCE

Danish: Do you want to play the 'cigarette' song? I still like to play it sometimes while driving.

Nina: Okay. Sure.

Danish: Do you remember how we used to sing it loud while driving. We were so crazy back then.

Nina: Not crazy, we were wild. Wild like animals.

Danish: Yeah, always high on hormones. Do you remember the first time I made you listen to this song?

Nina: Yeah! On your rooftop. In full moonlight. I remember it! I remember it all! Infact, that same night was the first time we tried weed together. For the very first time!

Danish: Oh was it? By the way, how is my poor baby taking the divorce thing now? Is she still mad?

Nina: Listen, I wanted to tell you something but please don't overreact.

Danish: What? Nina, I know it is always something bad with this tone of yours.

Nina: Okay. Okay. So, I saw Zibi smoking weed.

Danish: What? Where?

Nina: In her, her room.

Danish: How is this possible? Where is she learning all these habits from? She is just 14 years old for god's sake. What did you do? And where were you? I knew it! I knew you would screw it up. I should never have let her stay with you. Never! I will talk to her. She is just a baby Nina. How can she smoke weed?

Nina: Oh now you put the blame on me! Again! How is it my fault?

Danish: Then whose fault is this? Isn't she staying with you? Aren't you supposed to be taking care of her? Aren't you her mother? How can you be so careless Nina? Is this what she is learning in school? We are spending a humongous amount of our earnings on her studies and this is what we get in return?

Nina: There is more.

Danish: What more?

Nina: She was smoking with a guy.

Danish: What do you mean with a guy? In her room?

Nina: Yeah. In her room. And

Danish: And what?

Nina: And she was sitting on his lap.

Danish: What? Who was the guy?

Nina: Her high school senior. The one who used to come to our home for tuition.

Danish: Oh! I am having a very bad feeling. Very very bad feeling! That boy is spoiling my innocent child. I am going to talk to this guy! Why didn't you give him a tight slap? How can you tolerate so much? You know you are so lenient on her. It is all because of you that she is turning out into a spoilt child. And where were you? How can she carry on with all this nonsense in the same house?

Nina: It was during the office hours. But, that very day I came back home early because I wasn't feeling well. As soon as I entered the house, I heard giggles from Zibi's room. I went quietly and peeked from behind the curtains. And there she was. With that guy. Smoking the joint like a pro. I could not believe my eyes. I felt deep sorrow and pain and anger all at once. I was frozen at the sight. It was worse than a nightmare.

Danish: Then? What did you do?

Nina: I did. I did. I did nothing. I just looked closer. I tried to look closer from her perspective as she always asks me to. With open eyes. And there she was. Again with the guy. But, this time, I saw her happy. Very very happy. Ecstatic. There were sparkles in her round eyes just like before. How could have I done anything? I just held the curtains and enjoyed the sight of my baby's giggles and laughter for the first time since our divorce. And soon the whole sight turned into a beautiful painting from a horrible nightmare.

15. THE PAINTING

Rini: The bright yellow color at the bottom denotes optimism as if happiness is just next door, don't you think?

Meghan: But, the way I see this painting as a whole is somewhat away from optimism. The lady feels crushed under the burdens of societal pressure and her long hair stretched in the sky denotes a cry for help. She being a wise lady knows that it is not her fault, but the shallow rules of the patriarchy which can be blamed but she wears a smile on her face just because the ladies during that era were told to always wear a smile. And hence the way I see yellow in the background is its dark representation something on the lines of madness and betrayal.

Rini: Okay, your analysis makes sense but why can't we take yellow as a sign of optimism rather than betrayal? I mean, maybe she is hopeful about the coming years.

Meghan: Did you notice her eyes?

Rini: Yeah, all I can notice in her eyes is a sheer hatred for all the men around her.

Meghan: Exactly. It is hatred, hatred of extreme form. Under all such painful circumstances, how can one smile, even if one tries to, with all this abhorrence? But she does it. And she is doing that just to get a smooth escape from the situation because she wants to survive. If she resists, these men will boil her in that pot beside her. A lot of women would have given up by now and a lot of others would have resisted and showed their anger and would have chosen to get boiled instead of these tortures but the way this lady has stretched her hands with a mysterious smile on her face and hatred in her eyes denotes that she has a long term plan and is waiting for her day when she would finally betray all of them.

Rini: I think I get what you are trying to say. It seems, she has given up on everything, even on hope. Now, after this incident, she is no longer going to be the same person. Her one hand is stretched and if you notice her left hand has tight fists denoting oneness with herself. She is going to live only for herself if she survives and would care for nobody else.

Meghan: Do you think this painting is so famous because it represents a woman ahead of its time?

Rini: I think so. I mean I don't know if I am strong enough like this lady?

Meghan: Yeah, true. That's why this painting is timeless. It has the capacity to put all the coming generations of women into doubts. By the way, what is it that you wanted to share?

Rini: Well, the same old cries. But, I think now I have made a decision.

Meghan: Made a decision? Right now, at this point of time, without talking to me?

Rini: Haha, very funny. Yeah. Now, I think I am clear.

Meghan: Okay, what is it that you have decided?

Rini: I have decided that I will file for divorce. And I am very certain about that.

Meghan: Okay. That will really be good for you.

Rini: Meghan, did you invite me to the gallery and showed me this masterpiece on purpose?

Meghan: Did this painting help you make your decision?

Rini: Well, let's go out for a cup of tea?

16. INSTAGRAM

Siya: Mom, you don't understand. This instagram is like a platform where I have followers just like movie stars do. It is not at all bad, just something which is new in smaller towns like ours. See, I will show you, all these famous movie stars promote products on instagram for which these brands give them a great deal of money.

Mom: So, are you famous Siya like Priyanka Chopra?

Siya: No mom, not that famous. But, I have a pretty decent number of followers.

Mom: But, what do you do on this instagram?

Siya: I post my pictures, upload videos and promote products which I get approached for and in return I get money from these brands.

Mom: But, Siya, isn't it too much money just for posting pictures with weird poses? Shishu aunt had forwarded me one video of yours where you are wearing this tight top and just jumping around which you call dance. You should not post your videos like that, it doesn't look good.

Siya: Mom, forget about Shishu aunt, she doesn't know anything about the profession I am in. You will have to ignore these negative people.

Mom: But, Siya, you were so good in your studies, why don't you apply for a consistent job and settle in. This instagram is there today and it will vanish tomorrow, there is no job security in this. You can do that as a side business but getting totally dependent on it for your source of income is quite risky.

Siya: Mom, let me explore this space for a while. It is going well so far and I really enjoy doing what I am doing and it gives me a sense of freedom. Corporate jobs kind of bore me.

Mom: You never listen to me! Okay, show me how can I follow you? I too will keep a watch on what all you are posting online for everyone to see.

Siya: Here you go. Now, you can see all my posts.

Mom: Siya, I was wondering if I can post my poems on instagram?

Siya: Oh yeah mom, you definitely can. Which poem do you want to post as your first post?

Mom: Are there kids like you in majority who use this platform?

Siya: Yeah mom, teenagers and youngsters spend a lot of their time on instagram.

Mom: Okay, then we can post 'Blue Sun'.

Siya: Yeah, that is a great choice mom, it is one of my favourites that you have written.

Mom: Yeah, I know you kids enjoy craps more than the qualities.

Siya: Hey mom, look! You got the first like within thirty seconds of your post.

Mom: Oh, is it? Somebody read it and liked my poem?

Siya: Yes mom. Oh again and again. People are loving it, mom.

Mom: Show me, show me. Yeah five people have liked it so far. People are so quick Siya. Oh! Again! And see some Swapnil has messaged me.

Siya: Oh! Mom, see you too have admirers now. What has he written?

Mom: He has written-'hey dere, your work is LIT AF'. LIT? What does it mean?

Siya: It is a lingo mom, LIT AF means excellent.

Mom: Oh, should I reply to him thank you?

Siya: Yeah you can mom. Do whatever you want to do. It is a free world.

Mom: This is good, you know Siya. I kind of get what you were saying before. It is liberating. I will post one piece of writing everyday for the people to read.

Siya: Finally mom, I am happy that you got my point. Hey, where are you going now? Aren't we going to have lunch now?

Mom: Oh let's have lunch after an hour.

Siya: But, where are you going?

Mom: Siya,I am going to write more crappy poems to post them on instagram.

17. TWO YEARS

Mayasi: Okay Shrija, tell me what is bothering you this week?

Shrija: I don't know, I feel anxious these days. It seems I expect a few things from my husband and then become sad when those expectations are not met.

Mayasi: Do you convey to Ankur when your expectations are not met?

Shrija: Sometimes. Not always.

Mayasi: Why not always?

Shrija: Because I can see that he remains busy with his work all the time, and so I don't want to waste the little time that we spend together by complaining.

Mayasi: What is bothering you?

Shrija: I don't know. I don't really know. Sometimes, it feels all is good between us and sometimes, I feel lonely, and it feels pure horror. But, I really think it is all in my head. Things are all good between us. But, I don't know, somedays I feel kind of trapped. But, when I think about it, I always come to the conclusion that it is not due to Ankur. See, how quickly my mood changes and honestly Maya, I think the only problem is these mood swings, these mood swings kind of scare me.

Mayasi: Okay, let us not conclude anything Shrija. Let us just talk. Alright, last time you had told me that Ankur and you have separate rooms. Why do you guys sleep in different rooms?

Shrija: It has always been like this Maya. Ankur had told me before our marriage itself that our rooms would be different because he works at night. So, this is not new at all.

Mayasi: Okay, I take that. When was the last time that you guys had sex?

Shrija: Oh, I guess, it has been more than 4 to 5 months.

Mayasi: I am confused now. Has it always been like this? What about during the initial years of your marriage?

Shrija: Yeah, it has always been like this. I know our frequency is kind of low. Many of my friends have told me that. But, that is not an issue for me. I think the only challenge I am facing is that we don't spend enough time together. I don't feel loved. And now I have started doubting his feelings for me. Honestly, Maya, now I really don't know if he still loves me or not.

Mayasi: How much time do you guys spend together every day?

Shrija: When we take our dinner together. Around 30 minutes. Then, we do our dishes together and then we depart to our rooms. Earlier, we used to spend time together on weekends, but in the past couple of years, he remains busy on weekends as well. And most of the time, he is out on official trips. But, I can't complain because his business brings beautiful food on the table.

Mayasi: I don't want to ask this, but I really have to. Has he ever cheated on you?

Shrija: Oh! No. Never. I trust Ankur with all my heart. He is just a busy person, that's it. He is always on the calls with his colleagues. Apart from work, all he has is me and his only friend Trijay.

Mayasi: Does Trijay work with Ankur?

Shrija: Yeah, he had joined Ankur's business 2 years back. They have been friends for a very long time, from the time when they were in college together.

Mayasi: Is Trijay married?

Shrija: No. He is not married. Whenever I ask him to get married, he jokes 'I spend all my time with Ankur, I think that's enough for this life.' And Ankur also trusts him immensely, he discusses all his hardships that he faces with the clients with him because you know he can't share everything with me, I have never worked in my life and so, I would not understand. It is good that Trijay is his support system. He is like our family. Every Time he visits our home for dinner, we make him stay. They work together in Ankur's room. I also like Trijay, whenever he is around, Ankur really forgets all his stress and they laugh together on lamest jokes. Ankur is the happiest person whenever he is with Trijay.

Mayasi: Okay. Okay. Okay, do you accompany Ankur sometimes on his official trips?

Shrija: No, not really. Earlier I used to but not for a while.

Mayasi: Hmm. Have you joined him on his official trips in the last two years, you know after Trijay joined Ankur's business?

Shrija: No...I don't think so. No. Not really. Wait, what are you suggesting?

Mayasi: Oh! I am sorry Shrija, let's continue from here next week. My other client is waiting for me. I hope you understand.

18. CAGE

Nina: Okay, tell me one thing, what exactly do you want? What is it that you are struggling with?

Shimoya: You know, I really wish I was not born.

Nina: Ah well again, you did not answer my question.

Shimoya: "Now, please do not lecture me now on wishes and wants. Do you have any idea how it feels when you can see all your life right in front of your eyes as an observer and all you feel is pity for the character that is you. My happy moments were so limited that I could count those on my fingers and mind you, we are talking about 32 long years here. My childhood was ruined by nobody but my parents. I was lonely then and I am lonely now. I was just a pretty doll for them, a doll who they played with, a doll who they manipulated throughout. How could I be so foolish? My life looks so much easier for everyone from the outside but you will not understand that I was living in a cage my entire life without even realising.

Nina: Oh dear! Aren't we all living in cages? At least, you lived in a golden one!

19. MARRIED WOMAN

Meera: You know, I should not have married that young. I should have at-least finished my studies.

Krisha: You still can finish it, you know. And by the way, your tea still tastes the same as it used to ten years back.

Meera: Yeah, because that is what I have been doing for the past ten years. Making tea. And cooking food. And giving medicines to my mother-in-law. And finding my children's socks. And taking them to school. And running around them all throughout the day with a glass of milk in my hand. And packing my husband's tiffin. And changing my father-in-law's diapers. I am fed up, Krisha. I am really fed up. Sometimes, it feels like what I am doing with my life. When I see you and other women of my age going to offices and earning their own money, it crushes me.

Krisha: Dear, you can finish your studies and then you can apply for jobs. You were smarter than I was at college. I know, you can do it.

Meera: It is not easy now Krisha. I know that by heart. This whole house will crumble if I leave even for a minute. You know the situation, right?

Krisha: Yeah, I understand. I totally get it but, don't blame yourself for everything. You know, you were too young at the time of your marriage to think that far or stand against your family's pressure.

Meera: You know what hurts me Krisha? It is just that I didn't even try! I didn't even try to convince my parents. I don't know how I would get rid of all that guilt?

Krisha: Meera, I don't want to sound wrong but aren't you doing the same now? By not trying?

20. HIGHER PEAKS

Draney: Don't you think Capitalism is the chief source of our suffering?

Earl: What the fuck is wrong with you? Dude, how can anyone even think about suffering in the midst of this amazing nature with a breath-taking view.

Draney: I mean we have evolved over thousands and thousands of years as hunters and gatherers working together in a closed group, exploring the lands together and executing the plan together. And all of a sudden, after the industrial revolution, these human beings who have evolved to live within a group, were expected to work individually and produce results as quickly as possible. This whole drama of individual beliefs and individual dreams, all started from there and after executing it over generations and generations, we have come to a realization that although the per-capita income of individuals has definitely enhanced but what about our happiness? Don't you think our forefathers enjoyed their life more than us when they were always surrounded by their loved and trusted ones, their work-life balance was much better than us. I mean they used to hunt in the morning, would come back around in the afternoon after which the whole community used to enjoy the meat together. And that too, they were not required to go for a hunt every day if they are lucky in hunting down a giant animal. And what do we have now? This constant rush towards earning more money has definitely filled our pockets with dimes but has eroded the taste of life from our hearts.

Earl: Will you walk fast? We have a long way to trek till we reach the peak.

Draney: See, that's my whole point. All you care for is reaching the peak and what is your plan after that? What if you feel void inside you even after reaching the peak?

Earl: I mean, I have to reach the peak first to exactly know what it feels like.

Draney: Classic capitalism example.

Earl: Capitalism provides us a platform to dream, my friend. What is wrong in keeping a goal for oneself without the burden of what the community thinks and believes in and just keep on working towards reaching that goal? And the way you have portrayed the pre-agricultural revolution time period is totally biased. I mean, do you really think hunters and gatherers were living in a heaven in the lap of nature? Bullshit. Half of the time, they would be crying for their dead children. In the absence of Science, they would create all these stories of demons and fairies and all the other mythical creatures to oppress the weaker. Capitalism has let the Einsteins and Jobs and Gandhis flourish with their new revolutionary ideas that have shaped this world where two ordinary human beings like us are free and have enough time to trek and blame capitalism and enjoy nature without the fear of getting killed by deadly animals.

Draney: Earl, hey, look..

Earl: And have you ever considered taking infant mortality rate, life expectancy.. Oh! Yeah look at this beauty.

Draney: Peaceful! These two giraffes seem content in their lives,right? They are not in a hurry and enjoy even the basic thing - eating those leaves.

Earl: Aren't you feeling void inside?

Draney: Oh! Shut up! Don't try to spoil it now!

Earl: I think it makes sense what you were trying to say. Life is not about reaching new heights individually.

Draney: Uh-ah! Then what is it?

Earl: First, let's sit there under that tree and enjoy the view. So, if you really think about it, it is all about sharing the happiness of reaching peaks with someone. Like these giraffes. It doesn't matter if you are crushed in the pressure of the modern world or you are running around killing deadly animals in the jungles. I think we are fine if we have someone beside us to share our happiness and our pain.

Draney: Should we light a cigarette then?

21. MOTHERHOOD

Shani: Tama but what are you going to explain to your children? They will be devastated.

Tama: I know.

Shani: Why now? Will you ever tell me the reason?

Tama: It is not a sudden decision. I have been thinking about it for a long time.

Shani: How long?

Tama: Very long. For years.

Shani: For years? Do you realize what you are saying?

Tama: I know it is strange but what should I do? Everybody used to say that motherhood is the most beautiful experience that a girl can experience. Children are the little bundle of joys. But, I never felt that way. What should I do? Surely, I become happy when my children are around. But, motherhood has been taking a toll on my mental health. I think I don't have what it takes to be a mother. You know, right from the time when Rwishu was born, I feel shackled, shackled with love and affection and I have been living in constant fear all the time. My mind has become a mess, it is not a happy, peaceful place anymore. It is scary out here, very scary.

Shani: Oh dear! I don't know what to say. Motherhood is definitely the toughest job in the world. But, you can't leave your children. There is nothing like breaking up with your children. It is never an option for mothers.

Tama: I have been thinking for years now and I have decided that I don't want my children in my life. I am very very clear with it.

Shani: How is it possible? And Tama, you are not in the right state of mind, that's why you are blabbering such nonsense out of your mouth. I don't know if you will be able to cope up with this decision for years to come. You are a very good mother Tama. Why are you hurting yourself and your children? Just give yourself some more time.

Tama: How much more time Shani? It has been seven years now that I have been living in a hollow body. Motherhood is not for every girl. You don't realize what it takes to stay in my head. It is messy, heavily messy. I don't know if I have ever felt alive after I became a mother. And these emotions are something which I can't even share with anyone. How can I say that I don't want to live with my children? That kind of deep attachment scares the shit out of me. Shani, you will have to understand that I might die if I keep on living like this.

Shani: Tama..you should first...

Tama: You know Shani, what is the first step towards happiness?

Shani: No, what is it?

Tama: It is not simple. It is the word called 'detachment'. And detachment is definitely not easy for a mother because of all these messy hormones inside our bodies. But, I have decided to give away my current way of living where my happiness is all dependent on my children. I don't want to create a web of relationships around me where there is always a scope of suffering. I have never lived for myself. You know, never. It took me years to realize that I am not made up to be a mother. I know my children would not understand right now but I hope they would definitely try to understand their mother when they are adults.

Shani: So, what is your plan now?

Tama: The plan is to break free of this web and..and…

Shani: And what?

Tama: And breathe.

22. UPPER BERTH

Simi: I think this train will take forever to reach Delhi. Pathetically slow.

Uravisha: I know. We have no option but to rest and enjoy the train journey. There is nothing that we can do. Do you want to sleep? I will go to my berth. It is the upper one.

Simi: Oh! How can they assign you the upper berth? I will exchange the seat Aunty, it might be difficult for you. Look at its height!

Uravisha: No, no. It is fine. I don't generally go to the washroom once I sleep. And I am not that old. Am I?

Simi: No, no, if you are okay, then it's fine. And I sleep late, so it's fine if you want to sit here for a while. But, it seems everybody on this train has slept already.

Uravisha: Haha, yeah, looks like. So, do you study in Delhi?

Simi: Yes Aunty, I do. I am pursuing my Physics major.

Uravisha: Oh! Smart girl, I must say. Physics is not easy, dear. So, what are your plans after your graduation?

Simi: I don't know Aunty. My rank in the entrance exam was poor and hence I could not get any engineering branches and I am stuck with Physics now. But, this is my first year and they say if I get good grades, I might get upgraded to some other branches but there is too much competition.

Uravisha: Don't you like Physics?

Simi: I like Physics, it was my favourite subject while I was in school but I want to earn money too and I know I won't make money by studying Physics. You know Aunty, computer science students get the best paying jobs in the market and we get nothing although every computer science concept is nothing but an application of Physics.

Uravisha: Everything is Physics dear if you are judging it like that. See, right now, there is humongous demand of softwares in the market and hence computer students bag the best paying jobs but, money is not everything dear, knowledge is! You can take a different path dear!You can apply for scholarships and get admitted to the foreign schools after your graduation where you can earn money along with your research in Physics. Or you can do masters in some computer courses if you want to. You should not worry too much at this age. Is it your boyfriend who you are chatting with while I am providing you career counseling?

Simi: Ah..what? Oh, no he is a friend. And I heard everything you said. Let's see.

Uravisha: Just a friend? But, you like him, right?

Simi: Haha, I don't know. I mean yes, I like him but how did you figure out?

Uravisha: Because, that smile on your face pretty much says everything.

Simi: Oh! I should be careful, isn't it?

Uravisha: Yes if you want to hide your feelings but why should one hide her feelings?

Simi: That's because this guy is pretty dumb. I mean you know I am giving him all the hints but still he can't catch that I like him.

Uravisha: Then why don't you tell him straight away?

Simi: I want to but I need some kind of hint from him as well, right? We have been talking for more than six months now and I have no idea what he thinks about me. I mean, how should I approach him with that uncertainty?

Uravisha: Is he in your college?

Simi: Yeah, same batch. Wait, I will show you his picture. See.

Uravisha: I think you might have to take all the pain yourself and tell him that you like him, he will not give you any hints, I am telling you.

Simi: Does he look like that? Wait! Do you know him?

Uravisha: Yes my dear! I am this fool's mom.

Simi: Oh! Oh! I ..I don't know...

Uravisha: It's fine my dear! Don't be embarrassed. Trust me, it is absolutely fine. What a small world!

Simi: Oh! What are the odds? And I am such a stupid girl!

Uravisha: It is absolutely fine to be stupid at your age! But, I like you if that helps. Now, you carry on chatting with this fool, I will head towards my berth.

Simi: Good night Aunty!

Uravisha: Good night, Simi!

Simi: Oh! How do you know my name?

Uravisha: I just guessed it. I have heard only one girl's name from my son's mouth so far, so I figured it out. Did you feel butterflies in your stomach? Now, I won't embarrass you, good night!

Simi: Umm...Good night, sweet dreams! And Aunty...please..

Uravisha:Don't worry, I won't tell him about your feelings but accelerate the process, I must say.

Simi: Thank you Aunty! Have a good night.

23. HUMAN BRAIN

Mehas: That was the whole point of the play. Her dance in the end was nothing but a metaphor of how she kept on searching for a perfect soulmate her entire life not because she was not happy with the current partner but just because the process of search really used to excite her that something good is about to come.

Sumer: So, you mean to say that it was the excitement that was her driving force?

Mehas: Yeah, I think so.

Sumer: What I think is that her dance in the end represents nothing but her unsettling state of mind where her heart actually never settled with anyone and kept on rushing towards the uncertainty.

Mehas: Aren't we saying the same thing then? Basically, it was the uncertainty which used to excite her.

Sumer: But, how do you know if it used to excite her? Uncertainty is definitely something which we both agree on but I am not sure if she was excited to see what next is about to happen.

Mehas: Yeah, I get what you are trying to say. I have another theory of her being a sadist. She used to find pleasure in pain and hence she used to create such unrequired circumstances for her partner and herself so that they both go through the emotional pain. And her dance in the end on a painful music represents how pleasant and enjoyable that sad tone was for her.

Sumer: Yeah, that makes sense. I too was trying to figure something out in this direction.

Mehas: Yeah, and pleasure is something which is very basic. It is the need for pleasure which has kept the human race alive. It is ingrained deeply in the genes.

Sumer: But, if she is finding pleasure in emotional pain, why would she cry? I mean the way it was portrayed, it seemed as if she was very much disturbed by whatever was happening in her life. She used to blame her partners, friends, parents and everybody around her for all the atrocities in her life.

Mehas: Sumer, pleasure produces tears. You know a lot of humans cry after orgasm, I have the data for that. And this blame game for one's life is a classic action that the sadists perform. She did not know that she was deriving pleasure in those tears, she was not taking any informed decision. She was just a young girl in her 20s controlled by her emotions and riding on her hormones like a free cowgirl.

Sumer: Yeah, that makes sense that she was unaware of her condition and was doing everything unconsciously. But, how would you justify why she would go into a new relationship in the first place? I mean she is not getting any emotional pain in the beginning.

Mehas: Yeah, that's the tricky part. Basically, she unconsciously wants to repeat the same cycle. The emotional pain is her destination in every relationship.

Sumer: Hmm, so, she needs to get attached to somebody first then repeat the whole cycle again.

Mehas: Yeah, and if you would have noticed, she was never skeptical about the new person in her life. Basically, she just used to surrender herself to every boy in her life, giving in every piece of herself.

Sumer: So that it becomes more painful for her after their break-up? Yeah, basically, attachment is directly proportional to suffering. And she always used to be on the giver-end in all her relationships, so that she gets to blame her partner for everything bad that happened.

Mehas: Splendid! I think we have figured it out more or less. What do you think?

Sumer: I hope so. By the way, this play really helped us understand how complex these human minds could be. I mean their minds are tricking them all the time.

Mehas: Will you want to spend a few days with her brain?

Sumer: No, no. I think we are fine on our own little planet. I know our brains too need improvements but at least our minds are not fooling us and not giving us a disillusioned picture about ourselves like these humans' minds are doing.

Mehas: Yeah, it is like they are travelling with a monster inside their skulls all the time without even knowing.

24. BREAK-UP

Mom: Rish, would you come here for dinner, beta?

Rishyasi: I don't want to eat, mom.

Mom: Is something bothering you? You seem a little distracted since morning. Did something happen at school?

Rishyasi: Nothing is bothering me. I am alright.

Mom: That's the exact sentence you use every time when you are not fine. Do you know that? Try something new next time.

Rishyasi: It is just a little stress for my exams coming, nothing else mom.

Mom: Okay, if you say so. I have kept a few sandwiches in the fridge, feel free to grab those whenever you feel hungry.

Rishyasi: Where are you going?

Mom: Going to my room honey, I have to wrap up some work before I go to sleep.

Rishyasi: Mom, I wanted to tell you something for a few days. Come, sit here with me for a while.

Mom: Yeah baby, tell me what is the matter?

Rishyasi: So, I broke up with Sanky. And I am really struggling to cope up with that.

Mom: Oh baby! Come here. I knew something was wrong.

Rishyasi: Mom..I don't know what to do now.

Mom: Look Rish, heart breaks are hard, very hard. But, you will have to sail through it. Give it some time dear. But, I am sure you have taken the right decision.

Rishyasi: Mom, I really wish I would have listened to you. Why am I so stupid, mom?

Mom: Hey, take it easy. Don't blame yourself for anything. These things happen with people all the time. I don't want to lecture you with philosophical stuff right now. Should I call Misha for a sleepover, so that you girls can talk about it? Talking to your best friend will help you clear your thoughts...Hey, hey, why are you crying baby?

Rishyasi: Mom..mom...I have not been talking to Misha.

Mom: Wait, what? What happened between you two?

Rishyasi: Because Misha and Sanky are together now.

Mom: Oh! My poor baby!

Rishyasi: You know mom, I don't even have any idea for how long they were into each other, for how long they were seeing each other behind my back. How can Misha do that to me? None of them had the guts to tell me the truth. I figured everything out by catching them while they were making out in the back-yard of the school. You have no idea mom, how it felt! I felt pain, extreme pain, an unbearable pain. That sight was the worst sight of my life. And when I asked them, where were they? Both of them lied right in front of my face. Just like it was a habit for them to lie to me everytime. How could I not see mom? How can I trust them so blindly? I can get a new boyfriend but what about my best friend? I don't think I will ever be able to trust anyone now. I have lost Misha forever.

Mom: Oh Rish, do you want to take a break from this place? Let us go out for our little holiday? Somewhere in the mountains?

Rishyasi: Yeah mom. Please drive me somewhere. I don't want to face their bloody faces right now.

Mom: Let us go and pack our bags together, we will drive in the morning and spend some time away from this horror. Alright? Alright, Rish?

Rishyasi: Yes, yes, yes mom.

Mom: Look Rish, I know you won't get it right now. But, but, let me say it anyway. Believe me, believe me dear that one day you will look back at this very same day and it won't be painful anymore, not at all.

Rishyasi: How would it feel then, mom?

Mom: It would feel nothing, nothing at all.

25. MULTIVERSE

Snipa: Do you know what is one thing that always puts me into introspection?

Cenai: Let me guess. Is it... music from the rocks that is coming from the jungle behind?

Snipa: What? What is this dumb answer?

Cenai: I don't know. You have weird likes, who knows?

Snipa: No, it is this.

Cenai: This what? Sky?

Snipa: Yeah, dark night sky full of stars. It always makes me feel how tiny my problems are but how much unnecessary attention I give them all day long. My mind remains jumbled up with these smaller issues while there is a vast universe out there of which we know so less of. These are the bigger problems to solve rather than my stupid problems for which I keep on nagging all throughout the day, wasting my time.

Cenai: You know what?

Snipa: What?

Cenai: It is not you but this awesome marijuana speaking. Don't worry, I know you. You will not stop nagging. Nagging is just so much ingrained deep into your bones.

Snipa: I nag because I care. I care for everything that I do and I care for the people around me.

Cenai: See, I told you.

Snipa: Okay, I will stop right now.

Cenai: Do you know as per the many-worlds interpretation, every possible outcome happens somewhere in the other universe? That means there are infinite numbers of copies of you and I in the different universes performing different other possible actions allowed by the laws of Physics. So, in short, why nag?

Snipa: Yeah, that's kind of strange. Isn't it? I mean the numbers are kind of scary. Infinity has always bothered humans. How can one imagine infinity if one wants to? It is just so big, beyond our imagination.

Cenai: Try realizing it right now. You see these stars? Do these not give you a perspective of how infinity would look like?

Snipa: Yeah, kind of, but I just can't feel infinity like other numbers, you know.

Cenai: Can you feel zero?

Snipa: Yeah, zero is easy to realize. There are lots of voids in my life, you know.

Cenai: Yeah, I know. The biggest void is definitely the absence of Sunny.

Snipa: Yeah, right now, yes. But, you know, it is fine. As per the many worlds interpretation, we must be together in some other universe. Isn't it?

Cenai: Yeah, true. How do you manage to mould all these great theories so that they give you a small dopamine rush in your body?

Snipa: Aren't all humans doing the same? Moulding theories to create stories in their heads in order to get a small dopamine rush.

Cenai: Yeah. Everyone is hungry for dopamine. Okay, tell me one thing, what would you ask if you meet yourself from the other universe where you are together with Sunny?

Snipa: Oh! I don't know. I think I will be jealous of Snipa first and then try to observe their chemistry for a long period of time.

Cenai: Why do you want to observe their chemistry? For dopamine rush? But, what is that one question that you would ask this other Snipa?

Snipa: That's hard. Maybe. Maybe I will.. Okay, yeah I know what I will ask her. I will ask her the most important question that I want to know about her.

Cenai: And what is that?

Snipa: I will simply ask her if she is happy? After all this, if she is happy?

26. MY FRIEND

Shria: Hey, hey, it is my turn now. Just pass it on.

Zomi: You can't shout like that! How many times have I told you to whisper while we are smoking on the balcony? My parents can clearly hear us from their window.

Shria: Oh! They must be sleeping like a horse after that steamy, wild sex.

Zomi: Don't try to spoil my hit!

Shria: Zom, you think a lot! I mean they must be knowing already. They too have a smelling device called a nose.

Zomi: Oh! Do you really think my mom would allow you for another sleepover if she knew that we light a cigarette every night when you are here? You really don't know my mom then. She is not cool like your mom. My mom is not my friend.

Shria: Ah! You too don't know my mom then.

Zomi: Why? What happened?

Shria: Leave, let's not discuss our mothers' issues right now.

Zomi: Why? Sleepovers are meant to be bitchy. Tell me what happened?

Shria: You remember right, when I had told my mom about me and Drashal and she had seemed quite happy about it.

Zomi: Yeah, I remember.

Shria: No. No. That's the tricky part. She was just faking it!

Zomi: Would you ever tell me what happened exactly?

Shria: So, around a month ago, we were having some casual talks where she was telling me about the guys she had dated during her college days. I was having so much fun listening to her stories. In between these conversations, she very casually asked me if I had slept with Drashal. I mean what could I say? There was my mom telling all about her partners, so I too told her the truth.

Zomi: Then? What was her reaction?

Shria: Nothing. She kept quiet for a while and then said "I can't believe my daughter would turn out to be such a foolish girl." This was her exact statement.

Zomi: Why?

Shria: Basically, she believes the same what everyone else believes in. That, Drashal being seven years older to me is not serious and just having fun with a naive girl like me. She told me all these made-up stories of her friends where her friends had to go through mental trauma because they had invested their emotions in older guys. Can you believe that?

Zomi: How do you know that she made-up those stories? Maybe because she had seen those cases that's why she was just worried for you. I mean you can't blame her for that.

Shria: Oh Zomi! You would have taken my side if you would have heard those stupid stories. And anyway that's not the point. The point is why does she always portray herself to be super supportive and understanding mom when the truth is she really is no different from your mom. They both are pretty much the same. In fact, your mom is much better, at least she doesn't pretend to be somebody which she is not. She is what she is. Always.

Zomi: Yeah but you know I think you are exaggerating. She just shared what she felt like, you can't blame her for putting out her opinions based on her own experiences. Can you?

Shria: No, Zomi, it is not that simple. She did not just put out her opinion, she started intruding in my dating life since then. She started keeping an eye on me all the time, what am I doing? Who am I chatting with? And she started judging Drashal for all his actions. As per her, Drashal does everything just to get laid. Full Stop.

Zomi: Hmm, but that comes as a surprise to me. I used to find Aunty very cool with everything.

Shria: She is cool till everything goes as per she wants. And you know what, I broke up with Drashal a few days back.

Zomi: What? Why?

Shria: You can't get it! Can you?

Zomi: Because of your mom? But, she did not force you to break up with him? Did she?

Shria: You know what, I have realized recently that she always does that. She has been controlling my life right from my birth without actually forcing me for anything. She does that with a smiling face, you know just by being "my friend".

27. MEET-UP

Grishi: You know I was a little hesitant coming here and meeting you. The idea of arranged marriage kind of creeps me out.

Ramish: Oh! It is really great that you told me. I also kind of feel the same way. You had no idea how difficult it was for me. I wanted to bring this up but then I thought let your Ramen get finished first. You were enjoying slurping it.

Grishi: Haha, thanks for your consideration. So, what do you do in your free time?

Ramish: Well, there are a lot of things that I enjoy apart from my work. I play cricket. You won't believe looking at me but I like to exercise.

Grishi: You play Cricket? That's great. Who is your favourite cricketer?

Ramish: Virat Kohli. Do you have any interest in cricket?

Grishi: Yeah, I do. But, I don't play, just watch, not all the matches like my brother does but a few ones. Mostly finals.

Ramish: Haha, you are not a hard-core cricket fan then. I watch all the matches of India. Even test matches!

Grishi: Yeah, I totally get it. My brother too remains stuck to the TV screen all the time during the India series.

Ramish: I should get married to your brother then. I think we will make a great couple.

Grishi: Yeah, sure, by watching cricket all the time? Haha, sure. I can fix a date for you both.

Ramish: That's enough talking about me. Let us switch to a few serious questions now.

Grishi: Oh okay, Shoot!

Ramish: Okay, so, what are you looking for in a husband, Miss Grishi?

Grishi: Well, that is a heavy question thrown directly at a poor girl. But, no worries. I will try to answer. Well, I think, the most essential element I am looking for is support. Marriage, according to me, is supporting each other through thick and thin. I would support my husband to achieve his dreams and in return, I expect the same from him.

Ramish: Well, that was a great depiction of marriage. You seem very sorted in your life. I really liked that in you. I think I loved our first meeting. And don't worry. I just want to make sure that in my house, you will not be asked to leave your job after marriage. My mother too is a working woman and so, I will allow you to work as much as you want to help you achieve your professional goals just like my father did.

Grishi: Well..'Allow'? It seems, you did not listen to my expectations properly. I am looking for support dear, not permission.

Ramish: Hey, I did not.. mean to say that. It just came out of my mouth subconsciously.

Grishi: No worries, it happens. A lot of boys I have met before tend to put the blame on patriarchy for blabbering something like this subconsciously. But, you know, the subconscious mind tells a lot about a person because it does not allow the person to polish his words. Anyway, should we ask the waiter for the check?

28. OUR HERO

Tomas: Bro, tell me one thing, why is your happiness so much dependent on her?

Dilshan: I too am struggling to understand bro.

Tomas: Do you want to go out somewhere for a couple of drinks?

Dilshan: Do you think our prefrontal cortex makes our lives difficult? I mean, we keep on imagining things and building our own stories, craving to become heroes of our stories all the time leading to you know what? Disappointments. Huge disappointments.

Tomas: Well…

Dilshan: Well. Because our heroes are always ideal, doing the right thing all the time and getting rewards for their actions. And you know what, they have strong control over their emotions without even meditating for a single minute! Even on losing a girl, they rebound back quickly after crying for a couple of episodes. They won't be feeling this unbearable pain that I am dealing with. I too thought that this would end but I have realized it isn't happening any time soon. Life is much easier if you are a hero.

Tomas: Yeah. Well, stories always make us feel what it is like to be a hero but stories seldom tell us how to become one. Isn't it?

29. SIMU'S NANNY

Simu: You had promised you would play one game with me, remember?

Zoyuma: I don't remember anything like that.

Simu: That's why I had written a contract in my notebook. And here is your signature.

Zoyuma: What does the contract say?

Simu: It says 'Zoyuma will play one game of Super Ninja with Simu if Simu finishes her summer holiday homework before the 15th of May'.

Zoyuma: But, as far as I remember, Simu has not finished her Art project yet.

Simu: That does not count into holiday homework, Miss Zoyuma. That is a big project which one has to submit by the end of this year. Okay?

Zoyuma: Very well then.

Simu: So, should we play now?

Zoyuma: I have to follow what's written in the contract.

Simu: Okay, but don't tell mom, okay?

Zoyuma: And why is that? We are just playing a game that too after you have wrapped up all your holiday assignments in less than a week. That's an achievement which needs celebration right? Your mom would be very happy to know that.

Simu: No, don't tell her.

Zoyuma: Why is that?

Simu: Because then she will fire you and hire a new nanny for me.

Zoyuma: Why would you say that Simu? She loves you and every mom wants their first grader to have fun after they wrap up their assignments.

Simu: She doesn't want me to play. I know that.

Zoyuma: How did you figure that out?

Simu: She does that all the time. Whenever I am playing or singing or dancing, she scolds me. All she wants me to do is study and nothing else. And if you tell her then she will fire you just like she fired my last nanny. And I like you, not more than Rhasa but you too are good. I don't want a new nanny. Will you promise me not to tell her that we played?

Zoyuma: Okay, I won't tell her. But, Simu, your last nanny, I mean Rhasa had to leave the job due to some personal reason. Your mom did not fire her.

Simu: No Zoyu, no. I had heard everything. My mother had locked me in the room but I could hear everything. My mom shouted at her, she scolded her and then also hit her. She was crying out loud "Please leave me Mrs. Roy, please leave me. I am really sorry". But, my cruel mom did not listen and I too was crying and knocking the door from inside but my mom did not open the door till Rhasa left. I cried a lot the next day for Rhasa but she never came back.

Zoyuma: Why did your mom hit her?

Simu: I told you no, because she saw us playing. Rhasa used to tell me not to tell my mom that we play together, like ever otherwise she would scold both of us. And I never used to tell my mom because Rhasa was my best friend. But, that day, while we were playing in my room, my mom came back home early from her office and she saw us playing and then something happened to her. She became very angry and started dragging Rhasa down the bed and she dragged her till the main-hall. She was crying for help but I could not help her because I was very scared of my mom. And then my mom came back and locked me up in the room. But, I could listen to everything that happened in the hall. She hit her and used very bad words and then she slapped her. I was very scared that night. I cried a lot for Rhasa but my mom never called her back.

Zoyuma: Oh my poor baby! Come here. Umm..umm...do you want to eat something first?

Simu: Yayy! Pasta! Pasta!

30. BULLY

Alexia: Oh! I can't believe you. Why are you making that grumpy face at the end of every sentence that I am saying?

Mituda: Really? It is way better than your fake smiles and the color of your hair. Seriously? Green? That too parrot green? You are such an attention-seeker, but I am telling you, oh forget it! You are just too consumed in yourself to understand anything that I will say.

Alexia: Oh! An attention-seeker? What about those?

Mituda: Those what?

Alexia: What about the breast transplants that you have done? Is it not attention-seeking behaviour? Have you done it to make yourself happy? And to feel comfortable in your own body?

Mituda: Once you grow old, you make certain adjustments to feel confident, that's it! I have not done it to seek attention from men.

Alexia: Oh! Bullshit! I know you so well. So, don't try to give me all this crap.

Mituda: You think that you know me but believe me when I say this that I am very different from what you think I am. I am nowhere close to your assumption about me. But, I know every-thing about you, your thought process, your insecurities, your weaknesses, everything. So, don't you dare talk to me like that.

Alexia: Typical adult behaviour. Bullying a teenager to get an adrenaline rush for a while.

Mituda: Is it anything that you want to ask me? Or should we end this here? Because clearly it isn't going anywhere.

Alexia: Oh one thing, who are you dating currently? Please say..

Mituda: Oh! Okay. You are 15 right now, so you are hoping for him to be Shwetank, right?

Alexia: Yeah. Is it not him?

Mituda: Haha. You are such a naive girl. I am not allowed to give you all these details but I can tell you that it is not Shwetank. And please stop being so serious about him because he is clearly not into you. He will cheat on you with Prerna within two to three months. That hair is not going to enhance his feelings for you. So, start living for yourself.

Alexia: Then who is it? Is it Manu?

Mituda: See, how should I tell you? No, I am not dating anyone who you know. Basically, all the boys that you are going to fall for in the coming five to six years are going to hurt you because you don't see the substance and the values while choosing boys but you fall for their superficial aspects like their bodies and their hair. But, the priorities in your thirties become very different from what you have right now. So, in short, the person that I am dating is nowhere close to what you think he might be and you are going to change this fancy name very soon that you have kept for yourself.

Alexia: Yeah, might be because I am already bored with this name and by the way, you are such a bitch! You can't give me the details that I want and all that you are doing is bullying me for my life choices. Oh! Wait, which are basically your life choices. Why do you hate the teenage version of you so much? Can't you be a little sympathetic to your own younger self?

Mituda: Oh! You want sympathy! See, I talk to my younger self whenever I am angry with myself so that I can channel all my anger towards that version. So, don't expect any lovey dovey words from me because I know this is exactly what you seek for all the time, an approval from everybody around you! The quicker you shed this behaviour, the happier you will be.

Alexia: Wow! Claps! Claps!

Mituda: Okay, I am going to end this connection now. This is clearly not going anywhere.

Alexia: Yeah, sure, you can. But, one thing before I go, you know what have you turned into?

Mituda: What?

Alexia: You are behaving exactly like mom. Scolding me all the time and pretending to know it all. I hate her and I hate you. Bye and don't try to connect to your 15 year old version ever again.

Mituda: Oh dear! I wish you understood what mom was but I guess you will, you will eventually.

31. FRIENDZONED

Girir: Do you really think that is the case?

Dundi: I really think so otherwise, tell me, why will she ping you after almost three years. When you were approaching her like a snake all the time, she had outright rejected you even after everything that you did for her. I mean was she blind at that time? Why was she giving you all the attention in the first place when she had to friendzone you? I mean we all know she is not that naive. See Girir, she had rejected you because of Abjay and I am confirmed that they are not together now. Abjay is dating another girl from his office. I am telling you, she is lonely and that's why she pinged you. She was selfish at that time and she is selfish now.

Girir: So, what should I do? What if she asks for a catch-up or something?

Dundi: See, if you want to talk, it is fine but just don't get attached to her again. I mean just keep it casual. I don't want to tolerate all your drama all over again after she dumps you again for somebody else.

Girir: I mean why do you have to be always that negative? Maybe, she has just pinged me casually.

Dundi: Oh! Really? Nina pinging anyone without any purpose would be the last thing that one should think of. If she has pinged you, that means she wants something from you, let's be very clear with that.

Girir: Okay, I will keep that in mind. Okay, I am replying to her now. It is already more than an hour now.

Dundi: Okay. I bet she will reply back as soon as you ping her.

Girir: Oh! Yeah, she replied back. She says 'How are you? It has been a long time!"

Dundi: Now, she will try to check if you are dating anyone.

Girir: How are you doing this? She is just teasing me that I must be busy with my girlfriend on a Friday night.

Dundi: Tell her, yeah you are busy. Tell her.

Girir: Listen, I am not going to lie. There is no point. What if she wants to get back to me? I mean I want to keep my options open.

Dundi: Okay, then you will find yourself in the same trap again! And don't remain online for god's sake, it will show your desperation.

Girir: I am telling her that I am not dating anyone currently.

Dundi: What can I say? Now, she will try to make you remember some old memories of you guys together.

Girir: Oh my dear lord! She has asked if I still like vanilla more than chocolate? And along with that she asks if I miss the paranthas of our college canteen.

Dundi: Now, she will try to get to the point. She will try to apologize for not contacting you for so long and will try to tell you how much she missed you blah blah. Same old crap!

Girir: I can't believe it! She says "Sorry for not keeping in touch. I always remember the happy days that we had spent together. Crazy times!". I don't know how you are doing this! I am going now, meet at my place at 6 tomorrow?

Dundi: Okay, see you tomorrow. But, remember my words!

Girir: Yeah, yeah! Now, I have full trust in you. You know her more than I do. That is established today.

Dundi: Okay, Bye.

Girir: Dundi! Dundi! Wait!

Dundi: What now?

Girir: What would she say next?

Dundi: She will ask you for a meetup or something.

Girir: She has been typing for so long. Let's see what comes? Oh Dundi! I am enjoying it more than anything else. Looks like the tables have turned now.

Dundi: It depends on you. She is much smarter than you at this game.

Girir: Here it comes. She says "Hey, I wanted to tell you something. This coming December, I am.."

Dundi: I am what? Read it loud.

Girir: She is getting married, Dundi. She is getting married and she is inviting me to her wedding. That was it!

Printed in Great Britain
by Amazon

41125196R00056